This
Harry and
the
Dinosaurs
book belongs to

. . . .

APATOSAURUS
(a-PAT-oh-SAW-rus)

TRICERATOPS
(try-SER-a-tops)

SCELIDOSAURUS
(ske-LI-doh-SAW-rus)

TYRANNOSAURUS
(tie-RAN-oh-SAW-rus)

SCELIDOSAURUS
(ske-LI-doh-SAW-rus)

ANCHISAURUS
(AN-ki-SAW-rus)

ANCHISAURUS
(AN-ki-SAW-rus)

STEGOSAURUS
(STEG-oh-SAW-rus)

TRICERATOPS
(try-SER-a-tops)

STEGOSAURUS
(STEG-oh-SAW-rus)

APATOSAURUS
(a-PAT-oh-SAW-rus)

TYRANNOSAURUS
(tie-RAN-oh-SAW-rus)

APATOSAURUS
(a-PAT-oh-SAW-rus)

TRICERATOPS
(try-SER-a-tops)

SCELIDOSAURUS
(ske-LI-doh-SAW-rus)

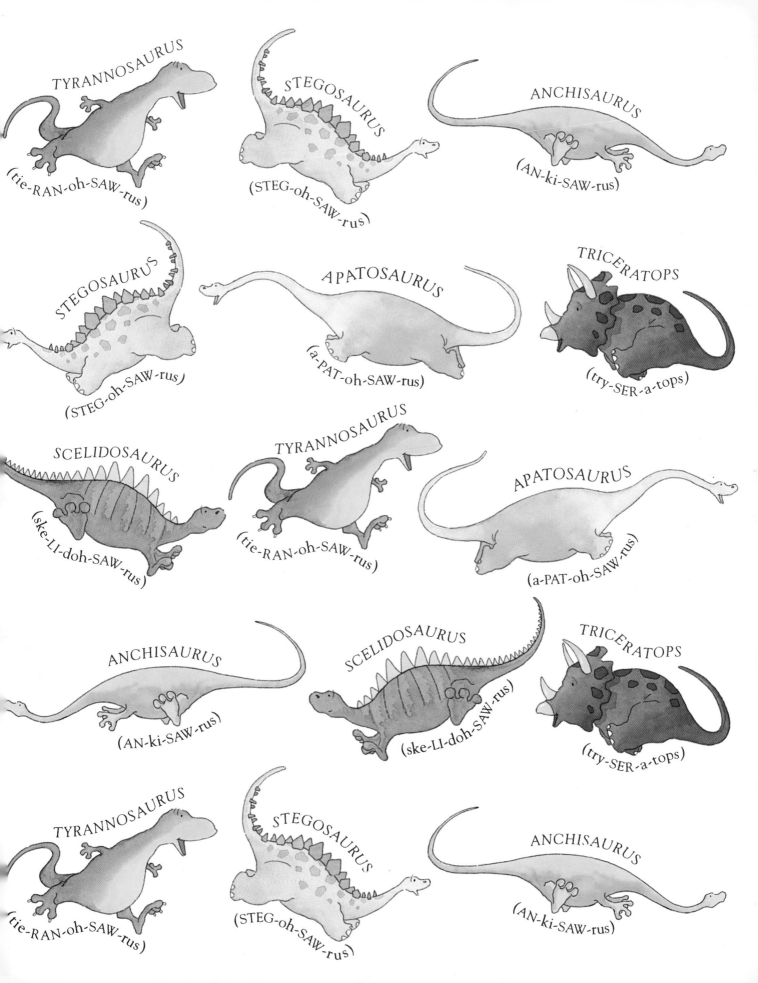

TYRANNOSAURUS
(tie-RAN-oh-SAW-rus)

STEGOSAURUS
(STEG-oh-SAW-rus)

ANCHISAURUS
(AN-ki-SAW-rus)

STEGOSAURUS
(STEG-oh-SAW-rus)

APATOSAURUS
(a-PAT-oh-SAW-rus)

TRICERATOPS
(try-SER-a-tops)

SCELIDOSAURUS
(ske-LI-doh-SAW-rus)

TYRANNOSAURUS
(tie-RAN-oh-SAW-rus)

APATOSAURUS
(a-PAT-oh-SAW-rus)

ANCHISAURUS
(AN-ki-SAW-rus)

SCELIDOSAURUS
(ske-LI-doh-SAW-rus)

TRICERATOPS
(try-SER-a-tops)

TYRANNOSAURUS
(tie-RAN-oh-SAW-rus)

STEGOSAURUS
(STEG-oh-SAW-rus)

ANCHISAURUS
(AN-ki-SAW-rus)

For Thomas Owlett
who introduced his bucketful of dinosaurs
to Ann and me one lucky Sunday afternoon
at The Chelsea Gardener
I.W.

For William
A.R.

With thanks to Dr Angela Milner
at the Natural History Museum, London

PUFFIN BOOKS

UK | USA | Canada | Ireland | Australia
India | New Zealand | South Africa

Puffin Books is part of the Penguin Random House group of companies
whose addresses can be found at global.penguinrandomhouse.com.

www.penguin.co.uk   www.puffin.co.uk   www.ladybird.co.uk

Penguin
Random House
UK

First published in hardback by David & Charles Children's Books 1999
Published in paperback by Gullane Children's Books 2001
Published by Puffin Books 2003
This edition published 2016
004

Text copyright © Ian Whybrow, 1999
Illustrations copyright © Adrian Reynolds, 1999
All rights reserved
The moral right of the author and illustrator has been asserted

Made and printed in China

ISBN: 978-0-141-37514-4

All correspondence to:
Puffin Books
Penguin Random House Children's
80 Strand, London WC2R 0RL

Harry and the Bucketful of Dinosaurs

Ian Whybrow Adrian Reynolds

PUFFIN

Nan thought the attic needed a clear out.
She let Harry help.
Harry found an old box
all grey with dust.

He lifted the lid . . .
DINOSAURS!

Harry took the
dinosaurs downstairs.

He unbent the
bent ones.

He fixed all the
broken ones.

He got up on a chair and washed them in the sink.
Nan came to see and say, "Just what do
you think you're up to?"

"Dinosaurs don't like boxes," Harry said.
"They want to be in a bucket."

Sam came in from watching TV.
She said it was stupid, fussing over so much junk.
"Dinosaurs *aren't* junk," Harry said.

The next day, Harry went to the library with Mum.
He took the dinosaurs in their bucket.

He found out all the names in a book
and told them to the dinosaurs.
He spoke softly to each one.
He whispered,
  "You are my Scelidosaurus."
  "You are my Stegosaurus."
  "You are my Triceratops."

And there were enough names for all the Apatosauruses
and Anchisauruses and Tyrannosauruses.
The dinosaurs said, "Thank you, Harry."
They said it very quietly, but just
loud enough for Harry to hear.

After that, the dinosaurs went everywhere in Harry's bucket.

They went shopping.

They went to the garden centre.

Sometimes they got left behind.
But they never got lost for long because
Harry knew all their names.

And he always called out their names,
just to make sure they were safe.

One day, Harry went on a train with Nan.
He was so excited, he forgot all
about the bucket.

Nan dried his eyes.
"Never mind," she said.
"I'll buy you a nice new video."

Harry watched the DVD with Sam.
It was nice, but not like the dinosaurs.

At bedtime, Harry said to Mum, "I like DVDs.
But I like my dinosaurs better
because you can fix them, you can bath them,
you can take them to bed.

And best of all, you can say their names."

Harry was still upset at breakfast next morning.
Sam said, "*Dusty old junk!*"
That was why Sam's book got milk on it.
Nan took Harry to his room to settle down.

Later, Nan took Harry back to the train station to see the Lost Property Man.
The man said, "Dinosaurs? Yes we have found some dinosaurs.
But how do we know they are *your* dinosaurs?"

Harry said, "I will close
my eyes and call their names.
Then you will know."

And Harry closed his eyes and called the names.
He called,

"Come back

my Scelidosaurus!"

"Come back my Stegosaurus!"

"Come back my Triceratops!"

He called, 'come back', to the Apatosauruses
and the Anchisauruses
and the Tyrannosauruses
and all the lost old dinosaurs.
And when he opened his eyes . . .

. . . there they were – all of them standing on
the counter next to the bucket!
"All correct!" said the man.
"These are *definitely* your dinosaurs. Definitely!"

And the dinosaurs whispered to Harry.
They whispered very quietly, but
just loud enough for Harry to hear.
They said, "You are definitely *our* Harry, definitely!"

Going home from the station,
Harry held the bucket very tight.
Nan said to the neighbour, "Our Harry
likes those old dinosaurs."

"Definitely," whispered Harry.
"And my dinosaurs definitely like me!"
ENDOSAURUS

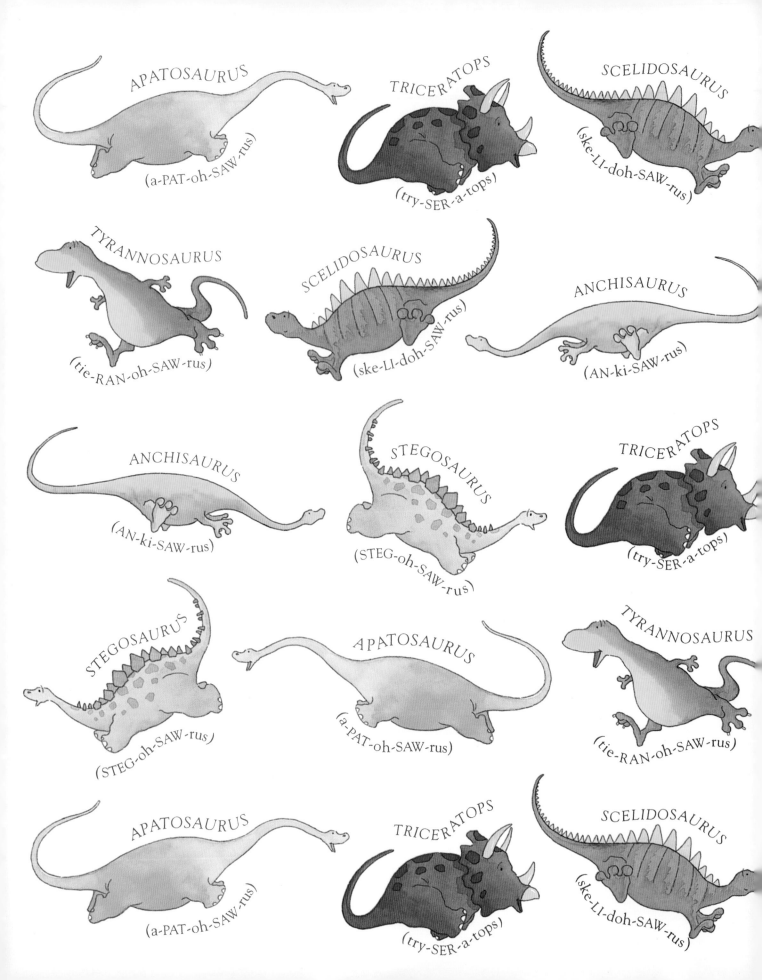

APATOSAURUS
(a-PAT-oh-SAW-rus)

TRICERATOPS
(try-SER-a-tops)

SCELIDOSAURUS
(ske-LI-doh-SAW-rus)

TYRANNOSAURUS
(tie-RAN-oh-SAW-rus)

SCELIDOSAURUS
(ske-LI-doh-SAW-rus)

ANCHISAURUS
(AN-ki-SAW-rus)

ANCHISAURUS
(AN-ki-SAW-rus)

STEGOSAURUS
(STEG-oh-SAW-rus)

TRICERATOPS
(try-SER-a-tops)

STEGOSAURUS
(STEG-oh-SAW-rus)

APATOSAURUS
(a-PAT-oh-SAW-rus)

TYRANNOSAURUS
(tie-RAN-oh-SAW-rus)

APATOSAURUS
(a-PAT-oh-SAW-rus)

TRICERATOPS
(try-SER-a-tops)

SCELIDOSAURUS
(ske-LI-doh-SAW-rus)